Broken Stories: A Quiet Walk Through Chaos

C.M. White

Broken Stories: A Quiet Walk Through Chaos

C.M. White

Published by C.M. White, 2024.

BROKEN STORIES: A QUIET WALK THROUGH CHAOS

First edition. May 19, 2024.

Copyright © 2024 C.M. White.

ISBN: 979-8224136896

Written by C.M. White.

Table of Contents

For those who doubted me, fair enough.

The Peak

The wind blew the mountain's icy viscera down the slope in slanting sheets that cut through the thick furs of the two men. Ice clung to their beards in clumps as they plodded through the snow, never looking at the path their snowshoes made behind them. Only looking at the path ahead and occasionally a glance at the mountain's peak.

Darkness fell and the wind didn't die with the sun. The stars were bright enough to see the peak of the mountain and like a choir of candles in the sky they lit the way for the two men until they reached their old campsite. The closest they'd ever been to the mountain top.

Sparks flew in the night as the flint struck the striker. Flaring the darkness away with sudden brightness. More sparks flew as logs were added and joined the night. The tents were erected when the fire was burning fiercely, and the two men sat near the fire to share companionable silence.

The old man pulled back his heavy fur hood and stared into the fire. The flames danced before his eyes. His hair and beard were silver while the left side of his face was covered in hideous scars. The younger man pulled back his hood, hair and beard trimmed short, little to no scars, confident, and often smiling. He wasn't smiling now as he stared at the old man over the flames.

"Think we'll make it this time?"

The old man grunted and looked at his pack sitting next to him.

"Making it won't bring her back, you know," the young man threw another log on the fire.

Sparks flew up and twisted in the wind. The smoke swirled and brought tears to the old man's eyes before he looked away. The young man raised an eyebrow but said nothing. The wind picked up and threatened to turn into a gale as the small fire flickered against the wind.

"We should leave," the old man said.

"Why?"

"Storm's pushing in. We'll be trapped for days."

"We should just turn back. Keep trying until we join her," the young man stood.

"You watch your mouth! She was my daughter, but you were her husband! Maybe she'd be alive if..."

The young man took two strides forward and drove his fist into his face. The old man fell hard, he wiped his lip and stared at the blood. He stood in the young man's face and spoke in a low voice.

"You ever hit me like that again, I'll kill you."

The old man stomped away and gathered his gear before he walked up the slope. He didn't look back. The wind howled and stung his face as he walked. An hour passed before his conscience nagged him and he turned back grumbling.

Halfway back he saw him lying in the open air between two rocks, one leg snapped in half. The young man was already frozen solid. He knelt and placed a hand on his cheek. Ragged breath sucked in the cold air. Minutes passed before he tore his eyes off the young man and looked to the mountain top. So close.

The old man strained as he shouldered the corpse and faced the peak. Each step was unbearable, but he found determination once lost and braved the lonely mountain on his own. One last look at the peak before he put his head down and trudged forward.

Hours passed as the wind tore at him. Each height brought a new valley. The old man struggled over another rise and saw only the dark sky before him and a black hump darker than the sky. He trundled up to it and smiled. It was a pile of rocks with a crude cross placed over it. he placed the corpse next to the grave and worked quickly to bury the young man.

He shrugged out of his pack and pulled out a snow globe, shook it once and watched the snow cascade off the very mountain he stood on now. A tear rolled down his face only to freeze. He placed the snow globe between the two graves as the sun was rising.

Not knowing what to do he sat with his back to the two graves as the sun came up. The fierce illumination painted the snowy hills in a bath of radiant gold. The mountain was sprayed with beautiful colors. The old man shivered. He watched the sun rise as he cried.

Painted Dry

Did I lay it on too thick? He thought as he watched the paint dry. It shouldn't take this long; he held a fan in his hand pointed at the door that was lying on horses. His face was one of boredom. A reasonable face for someone who watched paint dry. The dark blue was darker in the ill lit basement. The lights did little more than cast shadows. The same as his mind.

He painted because when he did, he didn't think. Not of the past, not of the things he'd done, the screams. Nothing but brush strokes. He found uniform and order to it unlike creative painting, a talent he was never able to fully grasp. Now doors. Doors made sense. Same with walls, ceilings, cars, and cabinets. Tables, chairs, stools. That made sense. Get them covered evenly, the most information you needed.

Painting made sense but when he had to wait for paint to dry, when the shadows were long and ever waiting, that's when the shadows of his mind crept forward. Oily and smokey, wrapping his head and pulling it ever down. He watched the paint dry and counted the seconds. Forcing his brain to ignore the smells and the screams. He expelled the thoughts of blood and death and counted. Thirty-seven. Thirty-eight. Thirty-nine.

He rubbed a hand over his thinning hair that was more grey than black now. He then ran a hand over the fully grey beard that only had one swathe of black in it. A curve that ran from his right ear to the left side of his chin. He could almost feel the wrinkles underneath the hair. He shook his head and replaced the hand to the fan.

The door leading to the basement opened and the stairs squeaked. Not willing to take his eyes off the paint or to move the fan, he called over his shoulder.

"It's not done yet; this has to dry before I can flip it over otherwise it'll drip."

He didn't know who he addressed but the footsteps were too heavy for his wife.

"Didn't Jenny tell you seven? What time is it?"

He still didn't take his eyes off the drying door. He thought nothing of it until he heard the hammer cock the gun back. Heavy hammer, probably a large caliber. Well, we always knew this would happen eventually.

"Will you allow me to turn around at least? Give me the courtesy of knowing who killed me. I won't stop you; I just want to know," his hands still held the fan.

"Put it down, I want you to know who kills you," the voice was deep and determined.

There was a chair nearby and he put the fan on it but made sure it was angled toward the door. Careful to the last. He turned and found no surprise in his murderer but neither did he find remembrance. The man was tall and had three-day stubble covering his face. He looked middle aged, but it was hard to tell, much younger than the painter. His dark hair was long and falling over his face giving it a shadowed look.

There was no smile, no glory, nothing worth remembering. A man there to do a task. Not different from a man changing the oil on his car or replacing an air filter or changing a lightbulb. Doing something that needed to be done. Taking out the garbage.

"Do you remember me?"

The man held the gun closer. 44. Magnum and held easy.

"Should I?" the painter asked uncaring.

He looked like he was waiting for a sandwich.

"You killed my family."

Again, no emotion. Just a fact and a task. A box that needed to be checked off.

"That really doesn't narrow it down kid. I killed a lot of people. Lotta families," he shrugged.

The first time the man showed any emotion. A flash of anger fluttered over his face and was gone just as quickly as it appeared. Replaced by the calm coldness that was there before. He lowered the gun and fired into the painter's knee. He screamed and fell to the floor clutching his leg.

"Think hard. Think real fucking hard," he cocked the big revolver again.

"You're that butcher's boy. I know you."

He gritted through the pain but didn't shout again. He was accepting this. Almost welcoming it. Almost relishing it. Almost. His eyes darted to the stairs.

"Your wife is dead. I used a piano wire just like you used on my mother. I'll shoot you like you shot my father. I just wish you had more family I could kill to make up for the lives of my brothers and sister."

"Do you expect me to beg for forgiveness? I was just following orders."

"My only expectation is to kill you and then enjoy a steak dinner."

"I won't beg," he said again as he clutched his leg and rocked back and forth. "I was just..."

"Following orders. The same everyone says. Does that bring back my family?"

The painter was silent. His back was to the drying door, and he looked to the stairs. There were tears in his eyes as he thought of her. His wife, beautiful Jenny. She pulled him out of everything, stopped him from killing, brought purpose to his life. And she was up there away from him. Cold and getting colder on the floor. Dead from a revenge that had nothing to do with her. She deserved more, much more than him. He shook his head.

"Answer me. Does that fucking bring back my family?"

The man shouted before he pulled the trigger and the bullet slapped into the other knee. It buckled and fresh blood pooled onto the floor. This time the painter stared at the stairs and bit into his lip, hard enough for blood to flow down his chin. He shook his head.

"It won't bring back your family. Or mine," more tears fell from his face. "Both of our lives ruined for something that had nothing to do with us."

The man returned to his calm demeanor. The chill could be felt coming from his cold veins. Pure ice. Get the job done, get out, steak dinner. The gun fell to his side. He shook his head and turned away before abruptly turning back.

"I refuse to feel bad for you," the eyes were red, and tear brimmed. "Fifteen years ago, when you killed them, I was ten. I grew up with nothing and no one. I looked for you, but everyone said you disappeared."

"That was my last job. I couldn't handle it. She..." he choked and looked away. "I don't want your sympathy; I was an evil man but repent for the death of my wife. There was no kinder soul in this world."

"Three years ago, I heard about a painter who did jobs cheap. Too cheap for the area, why would someone do that?" The man looked down at the painter's face.

"She convinced me to leave, to start a new life, to right some of the wrongs I'd done," the painter looked back to the stairs.

"I thought to myself, there's no way the Buffalo would move this far north. I mean I know New York has its moments but I always pictured you as a sunny beach type of guy. I figured you'd get sick of the cold and look somewhere warm. I spent two years following leads in South Carolina and Florida."

"I was the one that loved the cold. She was the warmth in my life."

He closed his eyes; he pictured her in his mind. She was beautiful and smiling. She was always smiling. He smiled.

"That surprises me. It surprised me to find you in Ottawa. Figured you would never leave the states."

"They're nice up here and neither of us had family. Our charities became our family," the smile stayed. It was dreamy.

"Another thing that surprised me. There's no way the monster, the butcher, the Buffalo would run so many charities. Almost enough for me to not even bother checking it out but I was curious on why someone would paint so cheap."

"I don't think of anything when I do, only when the paint dries."

"You weren't hard to find when I got here, everyone knew you. But you always were the craftiest fuck in the game. You always made sure you weren't tailed and always made sure no one knew where you lived other than trusted clients and close friends."

"Few enough of them but Jenny always liked company. She'd always insist on putting our best plates when they came over and she would always cook the best meals," his smile faltered and trembled as he thought of her. Fresh tears filled his eyes.

"I figured out who used you the most and got a job with them. I spent the last two years working at Wilsons Carpentry. But old man Wilson liked you and always would bring what needed painting over himself."

"Jenny liked him too; we were old friends. He's a good man but takes the charity softball game too seriously," the smile returned, and the painter looked back to the butcher's boy. "Damien. Your name is Damien, I remember you. They gave me a list of names and yours was the only one that wasn't crossed off. I always knew someone would come after me, I'm glad it was you."

"Old man Wilson had to pick up his granddaughter today and needed someone to pick up the door. He needs it by tomorrow and he reluctantly gave me the address."

"Not his fault he didn't know who you were."

"All this time. I've killed others to get you. Dozens," Damien knelt in front of the old painter.

"Does justice make it an easier pill to swallow?"

"No. sometimes I feel no better than you."

"You are though, boy. You are. I killed because I was told to, though the killing doesn't make it easier, you did it for revenge. One is not better than the other, but the one makes more sense. Promise me this one thing before I die."

"I won't promise you a fucking thing," Damien said as he stood.

"Don't kill another soul after tonight. If you promise that then I know my Jenny will forgive you."

"And you?"

"I've forgiven you the moment I saw your face tonight."

The gun was by his side, and he looked away before looking back abruptly and bringing the gun up. The hammer slammed forward, and the bullet slammed into the old painter's head. Blood sprayed the newly painted door and the old man slumped to the floor.

Damien looked down at the dead man with little remorse. The puzzling thing was the old man still had a smile on his face. Damien shook his head and reached into his jacket to pull out his cigarettes. He popped one in his mouth and lit it with a shaky hand. He inhaled deeply and he kicked the fan out of the chair as he exhaled. He sat down with weak knees. Fifteen years of work comes to an end. He breathed in the cigarette and watched the blood on the paint dry through blurry eyes.

Laundry Flash!

The bell chimed. Well. It clatter-chimed. The small bell that hung next to the door was broken and the chime was replaced with a small pebble. It never rang true but it didn't matter because it did its job. The job of notifying the workers that someone walked in. Clatter-chime again as the door closed and a tall smiling woman walked into the small building. Too tall. Ungainly, lanky, long armed, long legged, long neck, long gone look in the blank eyes like a chalkboard that had just been wiped clean. She wore a black suit that was far tighter than needed. Blue shirt, black tie, black spots on the shirt that simulate a Rorschach test. The smile was too wide, her hair was pulled back too far, too tight. As tight as the suit that made her look like a shrink-wrapped asparagus.

Her large saucer plate and milky eyes scanned the room. Machinery tumbled clothing both wet and dry. Clothes tumbling, soft rumbling in the air, the air much cooler than the sticky Southern heat outside. One corner has a small television mounted and is playing an old western movie in between static interruptions. Which were common enough but now were often.

The smile never left her face as she scanned the room with her large eyes. A few other people scattered about folding laundry, getting change, waiting. There was much waiting happening now. Three women doing three separate loads of laundry alone, a man with two children, an old couple waiting patiently and a young man sitting behind a desk reading a magazine. The slenderly tall woman sees this young man and her smile grows. She steps over long legged, overstepping, like a newborn fawn, like someone not used to legs. Or at least those legs.

The man looks over the rim of the magazine at the tall smiling woman approaching like a used car salesman from a cartoon and lowers the magazine slightly. He doesn't say anything, but an eyebrow raises.

"Hello," she says, her voice heavy with bass and a strange accent.

The magazine lowers an inch or two more.

"Hello, can I help you?"

"Yes...perhaps. Are you the owner of this establishment?"

Her eyes are wide and darting about. Her smile is unsettling. His skin crawls.

"Uhm. Something like that, can I help you with something?"

"You are not the owner of..." she peers at the business cards stacked on the desk. "Snow White's Laundry?"

"That'd be old man White, but he doesn't come around much anymore."

"Perhaps...I can talk to you instead."

The smile seemed to grow even larger. Like a wolf eyeing a barbeque lathered sheep.

"Maybe. Definitely depends. Anything business I gotta run through the old man."

"I am...how would you say? A...representative."

"Representing who?"

"Uhm," she nods at the magazine. "I represent that magazine."

The young man looks down at the magazine before setting it on the desk and leaning forward. His eyes narrow slightly. His lips pursed together. Skepticism incarnate. Once again, he looks at the magazine and then back to the strange woman towering above him.

"You represent Laundry Flash! the magazine? You?"

"Yes...something like that. We have much to discuss," a long tongue slithers out of her mouth and licks gently at her lips.

"You know what? I don't think we do. Also, look at that," he brings an arm up and points to his wrist where no watch has ever been. "Looks like its time to close. Past time."

"Sure...we'll be in touch."

She whirls quickly on one foot before long legs step her away and out the door.

Clatter-Chime. Clatter-Chime.

"Alright folks! We're closing up!"

Two of the women bundle up their clothes into colorful baskets. The single father bundles up his kids and clothes and makes for the door. The shadows of the night were long and moving. The young man thought he saw a lanky figure scurry away on all fours into the moonless night.

Clatter-Chime.

The father holds the door for his children and smiles as he holds the door for the two women. He waves at the young man and the young man waves back before walking into the sinking sunset.

Clatter-Chime.

The old man starts to stand up wobbly when the young man waves him back into his seat. The old man smiles appreciatively.

"We're just waiting for our clothes to dry. Shouldn't be more than a few more minutes."

"You're fine, no worries," the young man looks over at the remaining woman and smiles. She does not return the smile. His smile falls as he walks grumbling away.

"Uhm, excuse me young man?" the elderly woman croaks.

He spins and the smile returns.

"Yes, ma'am?"

"This is the end of the movie, and the static is ruining it. Do you think you could look at it for us? It should be over about the time our clothes are done."

"Sure thing."

He walks confidently to the small tv. This is one thing he was good at. The station was more static than western now and he had to drag a chair over to reach the bunnies on top. He stood on the chair and adjusted the antennae until a somewhat clear image appeared.

Zip. Zip. Shuffle.

"How's that?"

Zip. Zip. Shuffle.

"Ma'am?"

Zip. Zip. Shuffle.

He turns a skeptical head around and sees the crumpled bodies of the people who were just standing behind him. Their skin on the ground in suits with zippers shown prominently in the back. Standing above them are a group of reptilian aliens. Or aliens in the least. Bulbous eyes, antennae of their own, long necks, long fingers, long legs, weird mouths. You know? Aliens.

The young man lets a long sigh out.

"One of those nights huh?" he jumps off the chair and faces the aliens confidently. "Alright. Whose first?"

The aliens chattered and whined in their own strange language as their antennae twitched and their claws clicked. One took a threatening step forward before the young man bared his teeth and shouted something incomprehensible back. The three aliens looked one another and started chattering again.

BOOM! Stomp, stomp, stomp.

Something heavy landed on the tin roof and made heavy footprints as they walked. The three aliens and the young attendant all looked to the ceiling in unison and then back to each other. One alien lifted a claw and pointed to the door. The smallest one shuffled away and after three attempts successfully locked the laundromat door and turned back to the young man.

Stomp, stomp, stomp.

The walking was still heavy above but had slowed.

"Well, we're not getting younger. AGGGGGH!"

The young man screamed his war cry and charged into the midst of the aliens. The first rolled sideways and fell heavily into a washing machine. The glass broke and water tumbled onto the floor, spilling wet clothes with it. The second was caught in the throat with a fist. The choking became erratic, from his throat? Could just be the language. The barrier of languages was getting higher by the minute.

Stomp.

The smallest alien charges forward and the young man falls to his knees and slides in the water and detergent. A misshapen, sharp, brutal, otherworldly, deadly claw swings and scrapes the top of the young man's head. Just enough to draw blood but not enough to stop the momentum of the slide that brought him inexorably towards the desk. The first alien is up and running at him, the second is still choking and trying to drag air into its damaged windpipe, the third is running after him.

Stomp.

He looks above as another stomp creaks through the building. Then an awful squealing as the tin roof peeled away. The young man reaches behind the counter and gropes for a moment before the third alien grabs him around the waist. They both grunt until the young man is able to bring an elbow up and shatters the clicking face of the alien. Blue matter sprays the surrounding area, and the alien falls back screaming.

Stomp.

This time the stomp brought a foot through the ceiling. Then an arm ripped up the wiring, panels, and insulation until it was raining pink snow from the ceiling. That hideous face peeked through and snarled through an overly large mouth. Eyes now bowls of milk sans cereal. She clawed and snarled and shouted and spit as she rips a hole big enough for her slender frame to slip through.

The groping becomes frantic until that familiar ivory handle is felt. The chrome gun, if you could call it that, flung from the leather holster and pointed at the first alien who was almost on him. The barrel was chrome and half as long as a grown man's arm. Ported vents on the side glowed as the trigger was pulled snug as a bug and closer to the heart. A red flash and the first alien's head explodes in a bright flash, followed closely by a blue mist that floated about the room.

The tall woman has slipped through the hole and now long lizard tongue is lolling from side to side as her overly large mouth opens to screech in their own language at the other aliens. Presumably something like kill, murder, dismember, death, mayhem, and more death. Something like that.

Both aliens rush at him at the same time. The young man is able to shoot a bowling ball sized hole in the first. More blue goo spatters on the floor and mingles with the water and detergent. A shriek. A dreadful and painful and despairing shriek and the alien falls twitching to the floor. The second alien was able to knock the gun from his hands and get two claws around his throat. Squeeze, squeeze, squeeze. Like a human Go-Gurt. The air was being cut off and a rage replaced it.

"I don't need air like I need rage!" He shouts and slams his head forward making a mess of the antennae and clicking mandibles.

Rage and incomprehensible shouting continue as the young man's head slams over and over into the alien's face until there is little more than a mass of blue goo and jellied alien face dripping onto the floor.

"Good job...I knew you would...could...be better..."

She never finished because the young man screams and rushes her. The overtly long jaws unhinged as if ready to belt the king of all screams. But he gets there first. One fist grips the bottom jaw. The other grips the top. He shouts and she gurgles as he pulls with all his might until there is a deathly crack. Taught arms keep pulling until the job is confirmed done. The rage abates as he drops the slender woman. It rises again as he looks about the tattered remains of the laundromat and the thought of the work it would take to clean it.

"Bastards!" He kicks one and then the other.

He's suddenly so tired. So tired. He walks behind the desk and slumps against the wall. A few good blinks and he's out. Snoring softly and dreaming of tomorrow.

Clatter-Chime. Clatter-Chime.

The sun is shining bright as an old man shuffles through the door. Overalls hung together with wire hangers. Boots old and scuffed as they scuff the floor and shuffle through the mess of blue goo. He looks around and whistles softly.

"James! You about?" he shouts to the shattered room.

"Yea. Just tired."

The old man shuffles to the desk and peers down. The young man is covered in blue goo from head to toe. The old man chuckles as he looks about the tattered remains of his laundromat.

"Laundry Flash! was it?"

"Yea and they made quite the mess."

"Sure did. Well!" he slaps his knee. "Better get to cleaning. Good thing we're in a laundromat."

Night of Light

"What is love? Hah! What does it matter?"

"Seriously answer me."

"You ask me now? Bullets long marked for us and now coming for their mark, and you ask of love. Hah!" he walks away in a bluster.

"Goddammit answer me!" she's shaking.

Tears are there and full of frustration and fear.

He walks away in frustration. A frustration that quickly grows to anger. An anger that fans like a flame and a flame that catches a dry wheat field. Engulfed in fury he shouts as he fires the shotgun into a nearby pillar. The plaster crumbles as the pellets tear at the already crumbling foundation.

She jumps at this, and the tears flow true. The most truthful emotion she's shown in years. They aren't tears of fear for herself. The fear for her life was long gone. Stolen with her heart years ago. The tears were only for the lack of breath she felt for the imminent loss of her heart. Her love. Her everything. Her breath was gone and soon he would be too. She sits in silence.

"What do you want from me?" he suddenly shouts.

"An honest goddamn answer!" she screams back.

"What is love? What the fuck does it matter! Whatever feelings I have brought me here. In a big fucking mess because of a woman. A woman I would kill for. Shit, a woman I have killed for. Why? Call it love. Give it another name it doesn't change the feeling."

"And what feeling is that?"

"You know damned well what I'm talking about. That feeling that got us here. That feeling that made us play Bonny and Clyde except we always knew the outcome. They didn't."

"They loved each other."

He nods.

"I'm sure they did, and Tristan and Iseult loved each other too."

"And?'

"And Paris of Troy loved Helen. Bonny loved Clyde and Lancelot loved Guinevere."

"What's your point?"

"My point is pure love is destined to be tragic. Shakespearean love is destined in death. Romeo and Juliet died; in case you haven't read it."

"Why? Fuck the books and who writes them. Fuck the laws and who writes them. Who knows love more than those with nothing to lose but each other?"

"I don't write but I read and that's how it's written. Death and love. Love and death. Always depriving two souls from each other. It is what it is, and we knew the cards before they were shuffled."

"I would rather die than be without you. Already my breath is short and every breath without you would be labored and worthless. I would rather stop breathing than feel that pain."

He walks forward and sinks to his knees in front of her. Her head falls forward onto his chest, and he holds her lightly for a moment before drawing away. She looks at him with large eyes. Eyes of glass that shine through to her being. Nothing but love and devotion is seen glimmering back at him. He doesn't deserve it. But she thinks so.

"What is love? What does it matter? Why give it a name? I have lived and killed for you and I'm willing to die for you, which will be soon I imagine."

"Don't speak like..." she couldn't finish.

"It is what it is, and it's always been written for us. It's been written by God and author alike and pure love is punishable by death."

"Was any of it worth it then?" she sighs.

He pauses and looks confused.

"It was worth the world because you are my world."

"Oh!" she sobs as she melts into his chest. "Why can't it be different?"

Her question was rhetorical. He knows the answer. A written answer long ago that lead to this moment. And a feeling that hurt for the lack of oxygen and the lack of that person. A feeling that would get you to lie, cheat, steal, and murder. A sheet that would pale in comparison to the list of what you'd be willing to do for that person. Call it love. Call it whatever you want, it doesn't change the feeling.

"We'll call it love. Written or not whatever this is, it must be love. And I'll call it such."

"It always was and always will be," he smiled at her as the banging begins below.

"Last night. Let's go out sparkling."

She stands and walks to the old light. The one that used to guide lost ships safely to harbor. But sometimes it was just a warning not to crash on the rocks. The light was far past its prime after the new lighthouse was built. But the generator started up fine and before long the giant light was sweeping the darkness away from the worries of the night.

The banging continues from below. Muscles come to kill. Paid to kill. A check for love and two more lovers snuffed out. Write it down. One for the books. Done and gone. A light in the night suffocated by reality. Done in for love. What is love?

The light made its circle and like a cyclopean eye of the god of light it shears away the darkness. But not their fears. No. That would stay with them for the rest of their lives. She takes his hand, and they walk as lovers through the open door and onto the balcony. The banging is loud now. A creak and splinters fly upward. It won't be long.

He holds her close as they stare out at the vast ocean. The half-moon lighting the sea like a choir of candles. The giant light sparkling as it makes its revolutions. The soft warm wind blowing into their faces and streaming the tears away like rivulets of dried rivers. The hatch door is now splinters and angry men are climbing up. One shadow and then two and more are seen inside.

But the two lovers know nothing but themselves, the moon, the stars, and their love.

"What is love?" he asks her softly. "Love is a fire that is never cooled. Love is that thing that makes you do crazy things. Love is what I felt when I first set eyes on you. Love is..."

He chokes.

"You've said enough. Love is undefinable by most and impossible to define if it's pure. And our love is as pure as a mountain stream. I love you."

She leans forward and kisses him softly.

"I love you too."

His voice is husky with sadness.

"Hold me while we fall?"

"I will hold you for the rest of my life and long into the next one."

He holds her close as heavy footsteps walk cautiously forward. One step and a leap were left, and they were plunging toward the earth. They held each other close as they plummeted towards their destiny. One last soft kiss. A kiss that would last a lifetime.

It was written. Love is punishable by death. It was written. However not everything written is true. Statistically most love does not end in death and tragedy. Statistically most love is prolonged and protruded until more life is made. A surplus of life while the tragedy of pure love was destined at the start. Stories told and retold. The ending is the same.

Two hands are interlocked in a loving hold. Swinging between two beach chairs. The Gulf of Mexico is shining before them. More sun reflected off the pure white sand of the beach. The light is dazzling but manageable behind the shade of the glasses. A lazy smile is on both of their lips.

"I never thought we'd make it out of there," he says in a small voice.

"Maybe we didn't. Maybe we're dead and in paradise forever," her smile grows.

"Maybe. But I don't buy it," he laughs. "Paradise would be without discomfort. This sand is itchy, the sun is too bright, and my drink is empty. That's not paradise darling."

She laughs with pure joy.

"Maybe you're right. But you were wrong about one thing."

He sits up on his elbow as he looks at her. He tilts the glasses down so she can see his eyes. She smiles at this.

"What was I wrong about?"

"Our love wasn't destined in death."

"Well, that's a good thing to be wrong about." He smiles and her smile widens.

"I love you."

"I love you too."

Not everything written is true.

The Doorman

The door opened and the cool winter air flowed in with chilling integrity. An alacrity that uses big words to prove its worth. No one is confused, winter. The cold wind blew, and the door closed quickly. The man that stepped through was covered in a fine dust of snow. He wasn't out there long.

His suit was charcoal grey with dark pin stripes. The overcoat was longer than necessary. Flapping about below his knees as he wiped nature's dandruff from his shoulders. The bowler hat was slapped twice against his thigh and more grey sludge was added to the cacophony of despicable winter castaways. His black alligator shoes were wiped haphazardly on the soggy mat that was used to protect the marble floors from reality.

The man had a stern face. Hard for a man of his age. Seventy? Eighty? The wrinkles told the story but got the details wrong. His mouth was a hard, grim slit that seemed comfortable in that position. A silver Van Dyke beard with a sharp point was immaculately groomed. The ice in his beard and the chill from the air were nothing compared to the arctic blue gaze that took in the lobby.

He walked up to the front desk and unceremoniously dropped his hat in front of the two doormen. He then shrugged out of his coat and threw it on the desk next to his hat. He grunted as he did it. The older doorman, a man in his late forties was quick to swoop up the heavy coat and hat. The younger doorman looked on with indifference. A look that could be confused for insolence, which was exactly how the old man interpreted it as.

"You're our new doorman?" The old man said in a gruff voice.

"Uh-huh," the young doorman nodded.

"Then get the fucking door," he pointed at the door he had just walked through.

"Sure thing, boss man."

The young man hurried to the doors and pulled one open and was again greeted by a chill winter breeze that was surely overcompensating. Long legs stepped through. Long legs that seemed longer in the tight red dress that was revealing in a classy way. Her auburn hair was done up in a bun with just a strand or two tumbling down over her angled face. The eyebrows were sharp. Her eyes were intelligent. And her pouty lips were more prominent with the startling red lipstick that accentuated her face. God but she was lovely. Not just that, she was gorgeous. Drop dead if you care.

"Sorry about the kid Mr. Callahan. He's new but don't worry I'll..."

"He's new? He's new! I goddamn well know he's new, he just told me. But if he wants to keep his fucking job, he should do his fucking job," Mr. Callahan grunted.

"Yes sir. Of course, sir," the older doorman nodded rapidly.

"Come on darling. There is still much to discuss."

Mr. Callahan grunted to the woman as he stalked off to the elevators. The young doorman smiled at the beautiful woman, but she barely gave a look of disgust before she was past him and swinging her hips wide as she walked to the elevator. The old man and the beautiful young woman waited until the elevator arrived.

DING

The doors slid open, and they stepped inside. The old man hardly waited for the doors to close before he was pawing at the woman. The young doorman looked back in awe. She winked at him and blew a kiss before the elevator doors slide closed.

DING

"Man, what a prick," the young doorman said.

"Yup, but that prick owns half of Broadway. He buys and sells scripts and lives. You wanna keep this job? Then put up with his bullshit Danny."

The older doorman said as he hung the overcoat and hat up in the elaborate armoire that was exclusively there for the rich tenants to place their rich clothes. The young man, Danny Hope, was picking his nose as he nodded.

"Uh-huh. Put up with the rich old pricks bullshit. Got it."

He walked to the armoire before it was closed and placed the booger on the inside lapel of the long overcoat. The older doorman grinned and shook his head.

"I didn't see nothing, Danny."

"Let's keep it that way, huh Sam?" Danny smiled back at him.

Sam Kinney, Irish born, American raised, had been a doorman at the illustrious Florial Building for fifteen years. Everyone talked about New York and how it broke people. It broke Sam's father but was always kind to the young man who'd grown old. He was kind and treated all the tenants with the utmost respect. The same respect made sure he was tipped well. That generosity extended to bonuses around Christmas.

"Of course, but I need this job, Danny. Don't make trouble for me, huh? For my sake, Danny. We're just lucky that cowboy bodyguard isn't with the old man tonight," Sam lost the smile and spoke with sincerity.

"Don't worry Sam, I'll take care of you. You won't get in trouble and fuck the cowboy wannabe killer; I don't see him around."

Danny flashed the smile that had won over friends and enemies alike. It worked again as Sam thought of the resemblance to his own son. Sammy Jr. who would be twelve in a few months. Sam would do his part, but he really needed the job. That says it.

"I'll be taking off soon and you'll be with Sysco for the rest of the night," Sam said as Danny rolled his eyes.

"I think I'd rather have the old man as company than that asshole."

Sam sighed.

"He is an asshole. But he's training you and he'll probably be our boss when Terry retires. Which shouldn't be too much longer." Sam shrugged.

"Yea, Terry is old as time. The goddamn crypt keeper's grandfather."

"He's a good guy."

"You're a good guy."

"Hah! Says you. You wouldn't know a good guy if he pissed in your mouth."

"Some people pay good money for that. I'm just saying you'd be better for the position than fucking Sysco."

Again, Sam shrugged.

"Not for me to decide and I don't care who gets the position if I keep my job. Even Sysco wont fire me, the tenants like me too much."

"Even that old prick?" Danny asked as he nodded to the elevator.

"In his own way, yea. I think he does."

Danny grunted.

"By God she was a pretty one tonight," Sam said with a wistful smile on his face.

"Tonight?"

"Mr. Callahan has a nice young woman to keep him company every night. Usually, a different woman but she must have been something because this is the third time, I've seen her."

"Lucky bastard."

"Luck has nothing to do with it," Sam said dryly.

"I imagine you're right, daddy's money made money and his will purchase new homes for his dumbass kids. I got it right?"

"The gist."

BONG-BONG

The grandfather clock stood tall and proud in the center of the room and reached almost to the high ceilings that rose fifteen feet above. Sam checked his watch as if the clock was wrong. It never was. It was serviced by the same Swedish clockmaker that made it twenty years ago. He would die soon, and his son would tinker and work and die. Like father, like son. But that was only if the clock stayed undamaged. Sam checked anyway and the time was correct. He looked up satisfied with a smile on his face but when he looked at the morose Danny his smile fell.

"Sysco isn't that bad and it's just a few more hours."

"Thanks Sam and for what it's worth, you should be the next manager."

Sam walked into the back room and collected his coat and bag before walking out as he was shrugging into the heavy coat. He pulled it on and buttoned it. Sam shook his head once but there was a smile on his face.

"That's not up to me but for what it's worth, thank you. You're a good kid, you'll go far if you keep that temper out of your own way."

"Thanks Sam, I'll see you around."

Danny said with a finality. As if he never planned to see Sam again. He reached his hand out and Sam's smile grew. They shook and Sam looked at his watch again. The smile fell.

"The wife will kill me if I'm not home with bread and ham."

"Go on. I'll wait for the piece of shit."

Danny grinned again and Sam matched it.

"Try not to kill him tonight. Alright, I'll see you Monday. Have a good weekend Danny-boy," Sam had an enthusiastic smile on his face, mostly directed at the aspect of leaving the workplace.

Danny watched his friend walk through the door and felt the chill air whistle its cold breath through the lobby. Only for a moment but the cold made him shiver. More than that he heard Sam outside talking with someone and that could be no other than Sysco. Danny shivered again but this time for his imminent displeasure of being around an asshole for half the night.

The conversation in the winter air lasted as long as you'd expect a conversation outside in winter to last, except this was New York. The conversation lasted longer. Danny made a gun with his finger and placed it to his temple before he pulled the trigger. He used his other hand to simulate the splatter of brains. Through the glass Sam caught a glance and laughed before making excuses and walking away.

Sysco shrugged. The prick. And walked through the doors. The icy grip of winter was getting old, cold, and unwanted. Fuck the winter. Danny shivered again.

"A cold doorman doesn't last long," A grunting voice grunted.

Sysco brushed the would be slush on the floor as he wiped his coat, hat, and boots. Sysco was short and very aware of his stature. Napoleonic complex is the nice term, though Napoleon wasn't short, the not so nice term is 'short insecure asshole' but laymen's terms prevail. Danny nods politely.

"All quiet on the western front door?" Sysco laughs at the poor joke.

Sysco is short and mean. His bald head hidden under the cap that was rumored to never leave his scalp. The skin was taut and had the look of an elderly smoker, though Sysco was early turned forty. He grew a pathetic attempt at a goatee and looked more like a badly drawn sharpie tattoo. Any remark brought the wrath of Sysco and so all pretended to like him and his shitty goatee. Sysco disliked Danny on the sole reason that the young man was not afraid of him.

"How was Mr. Callahan's girl tonight? Same redhead?" Sysco blew out his cheeks and exhaled slowly. "She's something else."

"Uh-huh."

"You don't seem too enthusiastic. Young buck like you should be scraping the local tree looking at her," he smiled wickedly.

"Uh-huh. It's just a job to me. Not my business to care who brings who home."

The smile fell.

"That attitude won't keep you here when the old man is gone."

"I'm terrified. You should call him now and tell him about my insubordination."

Sysco took a step towards the young man and stared daggers up into his eyes.

"You know? I think I just might. Your bullshit has gone on far too long."

"I've worked here a month."

"Far too long."

The cold air broke the tension. The door opened and the cold air rushed in. Sysco immediately transitioned into the trained monkey he was. Danny took a moment before he struggled into a passably friendly face. They saw the first door close before the cold air chilled and stopped harassing the lobby. The second door opened, and cowboy boots stepped through. Alligator skin if you care.

Danny didn't. The man was heavy set and slightly overweight, but it was all fat on top of muscle. He had dark glasses on shaded maroon and a shirt of a pale blue sky. A tweed blazer over the shirt and apparently uncomfortable. The dark blue jeans and ten-gallon hat completed the ensemble The tall man tugged at the sleeves as much as he tugged on his scraggly beard. He was fidgety but not in an unseemly way. Almost as if that were his character.

"Welcome to the Florial. How can we help you sir?"

Sysco asked, not caring to see the ass he kissed.

"Goddamn it's cold out there."

He knocked his hat against his boot as he wiped the snow from himself. A few swipes before he tugged at the sleeves again. The blazer was tight around the shoulders and short in the sleeves. In short? It wasn't made for him. Why would a large man wear a jacket that small? Because he was told or because he stole it.

"Take your jacket, sir?" Danny stepped forward.

Sysco looked impressed but the tall man looked distressed.

"No thanks, just on my way to see my boss," the tall man smiled and made no attempt to take his glasses off.

"Who's your boss? I'd be happy to get the elevator for you."

"Mr. Callahan but I can find my own way. Thank you."

The tall man smiled but it was forced. Sysco narrowed his eyes and frowned.

"I should call up to your boss to let them know you're on the way."

Sysco was moving away when the man pulled a dark plated 38. special from his jacket and pushed it into his nose. He made a cringing noise that was cringe worthy to hear. A short squeal escaped before he shut up. His hands went up and the tall assailant looked at the doors before he snapped at Danny.

"Lock the doors."

"Sure-thing, boss-man."

Danny hurried to the doors and locked both the outer and inner doors. He walked back with raised hands as the tall man switched the revolver from face to face. Danny was calm. He even had a slight smile on his face. Real 'fuck you' energy. The tall man gestured with the gun back to the front desk. Danny walked to where he was told but he didn't cower. He left that to Sysco who was currently sliding under the desk to cower. He cowered well, Danny had to give it to him.

"What are you doing! Get down! He'll kill us both!" Sysco hissed from beneath the desk while waving him down.

Danny smirked and looked down at Sysco. His eyes widened and he nodded once to the desk. Sysco shook his head quickly. Danny widened his eyes even more and nodded to the desk. Sysco shook his head again. The tall man was not oblivious.

"Step away boy," The revolver swung in front of Danny's face.

"Uh-huh," Danny stepped back.

The tall man kept the revolver steady in his right hand on the young doorman while his left groped below the desk. The groping didn't take long, and the tall man found the sawed-off shotgun that rested on shelf. Very easy reaching distance for anyone and the tall man commented.

"Hah! If ya'll had half a ball between the two of you, you woulda' mowed me down at the start! Whew! Good thing ya'll some bitches."

He pulled the shotgun out and tucked it into his belt. The tall man looked left and right and back and forth. Danny stepped forward slightly with high held arms. The tall man took it as a step of aggression.

"Whoa, whoa, whoa. What are you doing there boy?"

"Well. You're clearly waiting on someone, not a secret, you're just that dumb. If you're waiting on someone, why would you have me lock the doors?"

The tall man smiled like he saw a checkmate.

"Because my friends aint coming in through the front door smartass."

"I mean I don't care but I am curious. Where are they coming in at?"

He nodded behind him. Towards? Danny didn't know.

"That clears it up."

"They're the cleaning crew. Should be up on twenty-two right now."

The elevator started its descent. It dinged as it hit each floor. The tall man was smug now. The smirk made it obvious, but the young doorman smirked too. This was concerning to the dull-witted tall man. He was the strong arm. Knock them about and keep them quiet. He'd done that. Less knocking and quieter. Yet the young doorman smirked. Why?

"Why you smiling boy?"

DING

The hammer cocked and sounded heavy in the lobby.

Sysco whimpered from beneath the desk. Danny kept his hands level and fully open. He shrugged as if he had no answer and that wasn't enough of an answer for the tall, dim, aggressive man. The tall man took two steps forward and this time the gun was level. Danny left the smirk. It seemed not even threat of life would diminish the young man.

"Do what you gotta do, but my hands are up, and I am complying."

The tall man grimaced and turned away.

"Then wipe that goddamn smirk off your face while you still got a face."

DING

Fifteenth floor and counting. The tall man was but his shoes were on. He paced instead. The revolver was cocked and re-cocked a dozen times as the elevator fell. Danny glanced at the clock and lowered his hands slightly before calling to the tall man.

"Hey boss-man. Can I lower my hands?"

"Huh?"

The tall man swung like Gumby as he leveled the gun. Un-cocked this time.

DING

"Can I lower my hands?"

"Sure. It won't matter soon; my friends are almost here," he nods at the elevator.

DING

"Just keep the hands where I can see them."

"Uh-huh."

The tall man walks to the elevator as it finally reaches the lobby. He's smiling. Sysco is cowering and the young doorman is walking slowly forward. Slowly walking to death but this time his hands aren't raised. The young doorman has his left hand in front of him and his right hovering above the small of his back. The elevator reaches the lobby and makes its sound.

DING

"Oh Jesus Christ! Did she follow us!" a woman screams as she stumbles forward into the lobby.

She's covered in blood, and everyone is unsure if it's hers or someone else's. She scrabbles at the floor as she falls and stands up defensively, pointing the MP-5 anywhere but safe. Two more men run out of the elevator. It's smoking. What happened? The men have hands on their knees as they breath. One is small and wiry with a scar across his throat. The other is of medium height with butterflies tattooed on both sides of his neck.

The woman assumes command and points her sub-machine gun into the young doorman's face. She shoves it up to his eye as she shouts.

"Are you with her? Huh!"

"I don't know what the fuck you're talking about," Danny says confidently.

"He's just the doorman," Tall man tells her.

The woman pulls the gun away and turns towards him.

"How do you know? How do you know she's not with him?"

There's a heavy whimper from beneath the desk and the woman turns back. She wipes blood from her face as she walks back to the desk. It's not hard to find the sniveling Sysco as she reaches down. She herds him towards Danny.

"Okay. Okay. I've done nothing," he said as he slowly stood up.

"What the hell happened up there? The old man was supposed to be alone?" Tall-Man asked.

"The woman was with him, whore I think, she defended him," Scar-Neck said as he hefted the double barrel twelve gauge in his hands.

"Old man is dead though. Definitely dead," Butterflies said as he slapped a briefcase onto the front desk and placed the M-16 next to it.

"Yea he's dead but that bitch killed Lee."

"And Simon," Butterflies added.

"Shot me twice and fucked me up with a knife!" the blood-faced woman put in.

"Yea both Lee and Simon are dead same with the old man. Did a number on Blood-Face over there too," Scar-Neck said as he nods at the woman.

"Did you get it, though? I mean fuck me all this…" Tall-Man looked at the case.

"We got it." Scar-Neck smiled.

"Well fuck me goddamn sideways! Hell yea!" Tall man punches the air in celebration. He continued punching and didn't notice the young door man step forward.

"Don't worry I'll pull through," the woman said as she was wiping blood away.

Both shots were shallow and didn't stay in. The cuts were bandaged as much as they could under the circumstances. Lots of stripped shirts and whiskey poured. Butterflies was checking her wounds as the young doorman stepped forward again.

"But we got it! We got the bonds!" Tall-Man was giddy.

"Old man had gold and jewels too. All in the briefcase," Butterflies nodded at the case that was laid on the desktop.

"Bless them but it was worth Simon and Lee," Scar neck smiled wickedly.

A door slammed on the other side of the elevators. Out of view. Emergency stairs and this would probably rank. It was enough to spook the bandits. They all reached for their guns and looked beyond the elevators. Butterflies pulled a Baretta from his waist as he crept to the M-16. The Blood-Faced woman walked quickly around and up to the elevator.

"We know you're there! We'll leave and no one else needs to die!"

"That's for me to decide!" another woman shouts back.

The Blood-Faced woman nods one way and then the other. Scar-Neck walks one way and Butterflies walks the other. Blood face steps forward and follows Scar neck. The tall man is hovering by the desk and looks nervous and that's the last look he ever had. Danny, the young doorman, pulled the 1911 from his waist and fired into the back of the tall man's head. Face, brain, and dark glasses fly forward from the force. The tall man's face still had one of confusion as he fell. Or at least what's left of his face.

The sound of the gunshot sends all parties flailing for cover. Danny dives behind the desk. Sysco dives next to him as the bullets erupt. Scar-Neck, Butterflies, and Blood-Face start shooting toward the desk. Danny waited until the thieves were out before he swept around the desk and picked up the corpse of the tall man, pulling the sawed-off in the same motion. Scar-Neck was first to reload, and he brought the shotgun to his shoulder and fired.

The pellets slapped the tall corpse and Danny fired the sawed-off back. He didn't see if anything hit before he dove behind the grandfather clock. Standing tall and proud in the center of the lobby and now it was safety from the bullets that spewed back at the young doorman. So much for the legacy of clockmaker, Danny thought as bullets slapped into the clock. Another door slammed from behind the elevators and that was Danny's time to move.

He rushed forward firing the heavy pistol and from behind the door another pistol was firing. The Blood-Faced woman was killed quickly. Three shots to the head quickly. Scar-Neck was still choking from the pellets that tore his gullet out. Butterflies was able to shoot one bullet through the young doorman's shoulder. It went clean through. The same could be said for Butterflies head.

The beautiful redhead walked around the corner and shot all the corpses twice more before she even recognized any other human. She looked up and saw the young doorman and she smiled. He gave a smirk.

"This turned out messy," she spoke.

"Uh-huh."

Danny walked over and viewed the corpses. They were in fact dead. He kicked one or two, more for satisfaction than anything. He was in fact satisfied. Danny put the gun in the small of his back before he walked to the woman. She threw the gun at the closest corpse and leapt into his arms with her legs straddling his waist. They kissed passionately while the dead stayed still, and the dying died.

"Oh God, I've missed you," the woman says in a husky voice.

"I'm just glad I can get out of this bullshit uniform."

They kissed again and he placed her down.

"Turned messier than we expected but we have the case," Danny looked around.

"With more than expected in it. We're alive and you're shot."

"It's clean. Check the case," Danny nods at the briefcase.

He then walks to the desk. There is a choking sound behind it. Danny walks cautiously and peers over. Sysco is choking on his own blood. A bullet hit him in the throat.

"Not your day," Danny says. He looks back.

"Lotta throat shots. You don't hear that outside of pornos often."

Danny shrugs as he squats on his haunches next to the dying Sysco. Sysco, to his credit, tries to speak. Both hands are waving spasmodically above him. Danny grabs one hand and shushes him.

"Sh. Sh. Sh. It doesn't matter now."

The dying man's eyes are wide as he looks at the young doorman who wasn't a doorman at all. Danny nods. Confirming the dying man's unasked questions.

"Yea. I got the job so we could rob the old man. Never expected all this."

Danny looks around at the corpses and then up to his woman. She had the briefcase open and was smiling. She shook her head twice before she looked back Danny.

"It's much more than we expected."

"How much?"

"Triple."

"Looks like we'll be sipping mojitos on the beach within the week," Danny smiled, and Sysco choked. Danny looked down at the dying man.

"We really didn't expect all this, but it turned into our favor. You really were a prick you know? I didn't want you to die but honestly, I think it does the world a favor."

More choking sounds.

"Don't worry. I'll be with you while you die, I think everyone should have someone to die with," Danny closed his hand around the dying man's. The hand went limp as a few more gurgled sounds choked up.

"He sounded like a dick," The woman grunted.

"He was a dick. But he didn't need to die."

"Not us, it was these shrimp-dicks that chose tonight to rob the old man."

"Bad night, wrong night, bad timing, dead night," Danny shook his head as he plucked a diamond from the case.

"Shut your poetic ass up, let's get out of here. Those mojitos are calling."

Danny held a hand to his ear, and he could faintly hear the sirens in the distance.

"Well Sam definitely gets that promotion now but if all else fails…"

Danny walks into the back room and puts the diamond into Sam's locker underneath an old shoe. Surely, he would find it and the good man he was he would sell it and give his son a good Christmas.

"They'll blame it on them, and we get away. Almost too easy."

"You call this too easy?" she says as she closes the briefcase.

"Uh-huh. Let's get out of here before the cops show up."

"You mean before we miss our flight," she smiles.

"Uh-huh."

"We'll have something to read on the trip at least. Seems the old man had a script on him. It's called Eight Shells," She wrinkles her nose. "What a stupid name."

"Uh-huh. Let's get out of here."

Gnomes Up

Kurleigh. A small cozy town nestled in the mountains. On the surface there was nothing special about Kurleigh. It was a place where families were raised, barbeques on Sundays after the game, children playing in the street, teenagers loitering around Carol's Diner, while the divorced dads played in their bowling league, and the divorced moms were planting honey traps at BBT Bar and Grill. An average place filled with average people doing average things.

The only remarkable aspect of this town was the vast number of stories that took place in and around the city limits. And consistently the stories would increase every year around Black Cat Day. Almost as if the black cats themselves were filled with mischief and mystery and strange behavior, that was the source of the stories. Almost as if there were a driving force behind these stories that pushed them towards a climax and resolution. Almost.

This story starts on the night before Black Cat Day. In the small and comfortable neighborhoods of Kurleigh the Victorian houses sparkled at night and the stars twinkled above them. All the families in the family homes were up late making treats for the black cats on the following day. While many of the younger teens and children were readying for the following nights mischief with a little pre-game mischief. The divorced moms were listening to Diana Ross and boat racing a bottle of peach Moscato. Their counterparts were listening to Bob Segar and having a few too many garage beers. This night was filled with activity and lights and cheer, that is, except for one house.

It was a Victorian house painted green with white shutters. This house was the only one on the cul-de-sac with no lights. Only the glare of the full moon on the lenses of binoculars staring out the front window into the front yard. This was the house of Stan Riley and Stan was the one holding the binoculars. He was looking at the cohort of lawn gnomes that dotted the front yard.

Someone had been moving his garden gnomes around. At first it was innocent enough with the gnomes being positioned in silly scenes. A picnic showing the gnomes playing frisbee and grilling mushrooms or other garden sundries. Once they were prepared into a game of chess and once into a football game. Silly, fun, and non-threatening. Until a year ago on the last Black Cat Day.

There was a fire, Stan was told at work, nothing serious but one of his lawn gnomes was burnt to a crisp. When he arrived at his home and found it covered with ash and firemen he was ushered over to the scene. The gnomes were huddled around and having a picnic with the focal point being a grilled gnome spit roasted over a fire. The gnome was all char now and the fire had been put out, but Stan just watched the burnt gnome turn over and over, spilling ash on each rotation.

There was little excitement after that but that was enough for Stan to install security cameras. That was the start. A perpetual roller coaster that would rise and fall like the ebb and flow of the tide throughout the year and almost always accumulating in some strange crime involving his house and his gnomes. That night Stan determined to find out who was moving his gnomes and why.

On the eve of Black Cat Day, Stan was inside his living room and staring outside as stoically as a scout scanning back and forth. His wife, Catherine is watching him by the doorway to the dining room. She sighs and Stan drops the binoculars slightly before tightening his mouth and looking back.

"Can we please go to bed?"

"Cat, you know how it is this time of year. I'll catch Frank this time I know I will."

She sighed again before shaking her head and walking away.

"Well, I'm going to bed. Come find me when you're done playing recon."

Stan grunted but otherwise ignored her.

An hour goes by in a blink. Stan took the binoculars away and rubbed his blurry eyes. He sighed in frustration and threw the binoculars into the lime green sofa that he hated. Every year with same stupid black cats and the same stupid Frank Zimmerman and the same stupid stories. Why did anyone care?

Stan flopped into his favorite chair and stared out the window. The darkness slipped by, and Stan fell asleep. He woke with a jolt as is phone was rapidly going off. They went off one at a time until they were repeated in rapid succession. Ding. Ding. Ding. Ding. Each saying the same thing. Movement detected.

Stan jumped out of his chair confused as the early morning rays shone through the front window. His fear and excitement ran together through his veins as he rushed to the front door. The phone continued its notification barrage. Stan put his hand on the doorknob and turned.

Ding. Ding. Ding. Ding.

Then, it stopped.

Stan opened the door stepped outside. The sun was still on the rise and mostly hidden behind the dark storm clouds that gathered on the horizon. The wind picked up and shook the maple tree in his front yard. The early morning dew fell off the tree and the wind picked them up and splattered them across Stan's green house. Some of the droplets flew in the wind and sprayed Stan's face. he reached up to wipe the water away and his hand brought back red. The wind blew again, and Stan heard a creak. He looks up and sees a garden gnome hanging from a noose and swaying in the wind. The paint was dripping off his hat and clothes.

Stan cursed and dialed the police. As he waited in his front yard across the street from him, Frank Zimmerman was getting ready to start his day. Beep-beep. The silver Beamer in his driveway lit up and Frank walks out with a steaming mug of coffee. He looks across the street and smiles.

"The black cat bandits strike again, huh Riley?"

"Go to hell Frank."

"With pleasure," he blew on his coffee before taking a sip. "I'll save you a seat."

Stan questions the flock and sends him the bird which only makes Frank's smile grow. Frank gets into his overpriced vehicle and drives off. Half an hour later and the police are there. Questions are asked halfheartedly, notes are scribbled, pictures are taken, but no one cares.

Stan was frustrated as the door slammed behind him and he walked into the house. Catherine is making coffee and frowns at the door slam. She greets him in the living room with a cup of coffee.

"You don't have to slam the door."

"No one cares about whoever is doing this."

"It's probably just some neighborhood kids messing about."

"I don't think so. Seems too.... nefarious."

Catherine rolled her eyes out of view.

"Well, I'm sure you'll find them soon. Okay let's get ready we need to be at the parade to help set up before eleven."

"Will Frank be there?"

She sighs.

"Yes, Frank will be there with Darlene. You know, I really wish you two would drop this it's been going on for near a decade now and it's getting ridiculous."

"Well as soon as he stops messing with me, we can move past it."

"Go get ready."

Stan showered and shaved and splashed cold water in his face as he looked through bloodshot eyes at the face staring back at him through the mirror. His hair is balding, bags had grown under his eyes, he wasn't eating as much so his weight had dropped and left him with more wrinkles. It was getting to him.

Keys in hand and all doors locked and alarms armed Stan and wife leave their home and drive the short distance to the diner where most people were parking. The set up took less time than expected and there was far more waiting around than anything. It wasn't long before more parade goers showed up and the crowd thronged the road on either side. Another hour and the band struck a tune and marked the start of the Black Cat Day Parade.

Far behind the band were the trailers filled with black cats gorging themselves on treats of Fancy Feast and Meowmix. The cat lovers were out in droves as they shouted lovely things and threw even more treats at the noncommittal cats.

"Stupid cats," Stan grumbles under his breath.

The notifications went off one at a time until they were repeated in rapid succession. Ding. Ding. Ding. Ding. Movement detected.

Movement detected in the back yard. Movement detected in the front yard. Movement detected in the living room. The living room? Stan looks to his left and at the face of his smiling wife. His kids were out, they were here, who was at home? And then another notification. Window broken, intruder alert.

"I gotta go, someone is in the house," his voice is erratic and tinged with something else. Excitement.

"Who? Why are you smiling?"

"I love you," he kisses her cheek and runs off.

"Wait!" she shouts after him, but he's already lost in the crowd.

Stan gets into his car and starts it with trembling hands. He's not sure if it's adrenaline, fear, excitement, or some conglomerate of the three. The car is in drive, and he peels out of the parking lot connected to the diner. He takes a right and speeds down the road. Six blocks to the house.

Ding. Ding. Ding. Ding.

The phone continues to notify. Stan doesn't look but his foot accelerates the vehicle. Five blocks now and now he's wondering if this was a good idea. Four blocks. Three blocks. Two.

Ding. Ding. Ding. Ding.

The phone is still rapidly notifying him of the intruders. He slows down to the speed limit and thinks the police might not be a bad idea. One block away and he turns onto his street. The front window is broken, and all the lights are on. And then his phone rang. Stan pulls it out of his pocket and sees the number, it's Kurleigh PD. Fortuitous.

"Hello?"

"Hey Stan, its Ricky up here at the station. We got two that belong to you."

Stan looks at his house and sighs.

"What'd they do?"

"Dine and dash nothing too serious but we'll need you to come get them."

"Uh-huh. I'll be right there but Ricky, there's an intruder in my house."

"Don't go in there Stan just come to the station and I'll send some badges out there."

Stan shakes his head slightly.

"Alright. Be right there."

Click.

"Good thing this isn't an obstacle."

Stan pulls into a neighbor's drive and starts to back out when he sees a flash and a window in his home blew out. Glass scattered and tinkled against a neighboring house.

"Fuck this. It's not like it matters, none of this, matters."

Tires squealed as pulled out and drove the half a block to his house. The car hit the curb with a bump and kept going into the front yard. Rutting up the driveway and sliding to a stop, the car was left to idle, and the door open as Stan raced into his home. He fumbled with his keys and dropped them twice before finally unlocking the door.

Glass covered the floor and wet footprints were all over the house. It was hard to distinguish one track from the next, but it mattered little as they all led to the glass back door which was shattered. Stan nervously grabbed the baseball bat he kept by the front door and cautiously stepped forward.

The footprints turned soft in the mud and ran into the backyard straight to the shed. The door was ajar, and lights were on. Hammers, grinders, files, chisels, and other tools littered the ground while the sound of soft singing and tinkering lingered in the air.

Stan stepped forward once and then again. He stopped hearing everything but the thumping of his own heart beating furiously in his chest. Quiet footsteps brought him forward until he was close enough to push the door open with the bat. As he did the singing stopped and the tinkering slowed to a trickle. Led on built courage Stan screams his war cry and charges into the shed and is immediately knocked unconscious.

Stan woke to a light swinging over his head. He tried to rub his face but realized his hands were tied. He looked down and saw his whole body was tied up with extension cords. As his vision began to focus, he saw he was surrounded by small figures with pointed heads. Stan shook his head and saw he was surrounded by his garden gnomes.

"Blyat."

The gnomes moved out of the way and a gnome known as Frankie Crisp strode down the isle of gnomes to face Stan Riley.

"It is very unfortunate that it had to come to this Mr. Riley," the gnome spoke with a thick Russian accent.

"Frankie Crisp. Why? How? I bought you from some old man in Rhode Island."

"Yes, that is what happened, but my comrades and I have been working on this for a long time. Now it is time to strike at the heart of capitalism. Now we will seize the means of production and..."

The door kicked open and Frank Zimmerman stood holding a shovel. The smile on his face was infectious enough to make Stan smile.

"Spokoiny nochi comrades, welcome to America."

He rushed into the room swinging the shovel like a battle-axe on an ancient battlefield. The gnomes screamed their challenge and rushed at him with knives and hammers. Stan was tipped over in the excitement and didn't see much of the action. A gnome flew here and there. Pieces of ceramic shattered and sprayed the room.

The battle didn't last long before Stan saw the smiling face of Frank kneeling over him. Stan was untied and Frank helped him to his feet. The carnage of the gnomes was scattered across the room. Frank leaned on the shovel.

"What..."

"Special Agent Ross with the FBI. We've been looking for these Russian dwarfs that were illegally smuggled into the country as an act to overthrow the government. I've been following these little bastards for years."

"Is that why you pretended to hate me all these years?"

Frank laughed loudly.

"No, I just don't like you."

Dasvidaniya.

Half Century Hatred

Piercing blue eyes stared back at him. Surrounded by wrinkled and sallow skin and peppered with liver spots. His hair was thinning and white as a mountain top, it was combed over to the tail which was his long and lank hair that ran down the length of his back and stopping just below the shoulder blades.

The years had washed over him like the ocean breaking a mountain. It showed. But the eyes were as sharp as ever. He stared at himself in the mirror and hardly recognized the grizzly appearance that included slanting eyes and a scowl.

"I have taken too much enjoyment in hatred."

At that, the salted face cracked into a grin. His only smile for the day until he was home again. Quickly and effortlessly, he slipped back into his 'normal' face. The frown that was famous on the shore to all known and unknown ruffians.

His walk was still uninhibited besides the slight limp in his right leg, a parting gift of shrapnel from a war long ago. Most days it was hardly noticeable, depending on circumstances. The circumstances: cold weather, pure rage, and uncontrollable sadness. He knew from experience.

His limp was barely noticeable today as he walked down the narrow hallway of his small house, stopping just before the coat rack. His hands reached forward and took the cardigan and flat cap off their respective hooks. His hands did this with hardly a tremor. Yet another thing I'm better at, he thought smugly.

The hat fit snugly on his head as it had every morning for the last seventeen years. Seventeen years and three mornings before, his favorite hat was burned after his rival snatched it off his head in a physical fight. That had been the talk of their small coastal town. The talk lasted for five years.

People age and forget. They move and shift and find another chatter alarm. And so, it was and as it was, so it went. But the names Charlie Stratton and Jim 'Boogie' Janson, in this small community, were never far from anyone's lips. They hated each other and that hatred had spanned over five decades. Fifty years of hatred, so long ago that the small town of Bricksford, Maine, had filled and refilled twice. So long ago, that no one remembered why they hated each other. But they knew.

The inhabitants of the lonely coastal city of Bricksford were mostly elderly and the youngsters replaced the elderly. However, the youngsters were never younger than forty. The town died and filled and died again. It was filling itself up again but the hatred between the two old men never abated. Their anger never sated. The feud lived and was always the lively talk of the town.

Now, Jim Janson looks down at his loafers and sees the dog. It's elderly as well. A white face and silver hair, which could have easily been the way he was born; however, it was so long ago that Jim doesn't remember. Memory is fickle. Some things are welded, and others are glued. Some memories hold and others fade with time.

The welded memory was when he brought the puppy home. His wife and three daughters screeched with happiness, while his sons' played soldiers in the backyard. What was its color though? Sticky glue memory. He shook his head and the dog whined.

"Don't you whine at me boy!"

It was gruffer than he intended, and the dog hunched closer to the floor. Like a molten crust; hard exterior, gushy inside. His heart twinged and he grunted at the dog, his form of affection. The dog sat up quickly for its old age, tongue lagging, content with the conveyed message.

"Of course ya comin with me. You got nowhere else to go."

He opened the door and walked outside. The dog followed him and trudged away to stand beside the small garage that held the Patina colored truck that looked far worse than it ran. It ran with a loving touch tinkered by a hateful man. Jim only loved his dog more than his truck. His wife before that but she left and is inconsequential now. Dog, truck, kids, and welding.

The kids were old. Forty-five or more. Among the five of them he was responsible for over two centuries. They had their own families now and called him once on his birthday, once on Father's Day, and once on Christmas. Visits were limited to one family per year but were spaced out. To preserve feelings or whatever. Almost exactly two and half months would go by before a plump, smiling, fake, family would show up.

Their plump fingers would touch all of the surfaces of the house and the dog would hide. They would smile and be fake and check his health or rather check the health of the inheritance. The money. The division and articulation and planning. All for the money. Money never made people monsters. Money was the knife in the hands of monsters. What's the monetary value of a backstab?

Humans have always been monsters; it's just more publicized now. Facts people care less about these days but facts, nonetheless. Humans were responsible for Hiroshima, Nanking, Khartoum, Jerusalem, and the Bricksford Recreational Center. The latter in Jim's mind was above or beyond equal after the stint that Charlie pulled seven years prior.

After retirement the activities became an active part of most people's lives in Bricksford. And the epicenter of all these activities was, of course, the Bricksford Recreational Center. This was where bingo, keno, and squash were played. Wrinkled bodies steamed in the saunas after sweating on the meticulously kept golf course or the red dirt tennis courts. They never explained the reasoning for flat red dirt on the tennis courts beyond "the look".

This was Boogie's 'holy place' until Charlie Stratton stole the contract to maintain the lawns from him. On an average week that was his cathartic time. A thin cigar clenched between his mouth like a slight slit in tanned granite. A cold beer in the cupholder and the wind and music of Steve Winwood blowing wildly around his ears. The closest he came to happiness, behind anytime he showed up his rival.

The day the contract was signed was the last time Jim 'Boogie' Janson ever set foot on the premises. An oath he had kept for seven years. An oath he was prepared to die with. That thought made him want to smile. But he didn't. He never smiled in public.

Jim opened the shed door before walking slowly in and slowly opening the door to the old truck. He straightened the rearview and he caught his own reflection. What an old fu...

The dog barked and Jim blinked. He reached for the key above the visor and stuck it into the ignition. The truck started on the first try and with hardly a glance he backed the truck out far enough to close the garage door.

Jim then left the truck running and slowly closed the door as the dog waited patiently. The door closed and locked, and the dog looked on indifferently; he knew his time would come. Jim walks carefully to the passenger side and at last the dog shows his excitement. Tail wagging and again on four legs. Jim opens the door and whistles. The dog is nearly as slow as he is and after the years the dog needs a little boost to get into the truck. Boogie does this unquestioning.

The dog needs less help getting into the seat and Jim slowly makes his way back to the driver's side. He takes his archaic time unlocking the door and climbing in. The reason he always locked the truck door, in a town where crime was virtually nonexistent, was of course, because of his nemesis. Twenty years prior, Charlie Stratton, had stolen his truck and with a heavy rock behind the acceleration set it on course for the cold Atlantic waters. Fair is fair however because that stint was done in retaliation for Jim setting fire to Charlie's beloved Harley.

Their crimes varied from mildly mischievous to blatant larceny, arson, and damage to property. Although, through the hatred they shared a bond. The bond of not talking to people who just weren't simply minding their business. Anyone who asked a question to either party of the infamous Bricksford Feud received the same answer.

"Mind your fucking business."

Thoughts of past wrongs burned him up inside. But it was a good burn. Like the slow burn of incense and the curling smoke filling his body with content. He shook his head once and pulled out of the drive.

The traffic was light for the early afternoon and as he drove Jim looked at the locations of dozens of altercations and each one brought on a memory. Memories of being young and strong. Memories of being old and weak. Memories of those dead and gone. But underneath it all the memories of so pleasurably hating someone for over fifty years.

The drive was short and up ahead Jim saw his destination. An old pub named the *Salted Buck*, the local watering hole where the majority of the old men in the old town came to congregate, contemplate, and complain about their wives. One of the major sources of entertainment was the latest news on the feud.

So, on this day when one of the old regulars saw the patina truck turning into the half-crumbled parking lot, he threw down his half-smoked cigar and went running into the pub. The term 'running' is generous as the old man went forward at a fast shuffle. The equivalent of running in Bricksford.

Jim thought nothing of this. This was a similar reaction he received anytime he rolled up to the *Buck*. Man, and dog took their time getting out of the truck before making the slow journey to the front door, after locking the truck, of course. Above the door was a once green sign with a picture of a prancing buck and underneath in Gothic letters read: *The Salted Buck*.

Jim pushed the glass door open to silence. Not true silence, mind you. There were murmurings, drinks were still being poured and the slurps accompanied them. And underneath it all like a soft sheet was the haunting sound of *Danny Boy*. Sung beautifully and low. Eyes turned to Jim as he walked in.

He ignored the inquisitive stares and anyone who approached him. He waved them all away. Jim never talked to anyone until he had his seven and seven and draft of the local sour. Just as sour and always on time was the bartender, Todd Kirkland, he placed the drinks in front of a retired salesman. The salesman perked up when he saw the drinks but when he turned around his smile fell. The salesman got up and nodded respectfully to Jim and gave him his seat.

Jim grunted as he sat down. He took a drink from each and gave a small sigh after both. He looked up and Todd hadn't moved, his usual sour face was even more prominent today. The bartender looked left and right at the raised eyebrows and the piercing silence.

"Tend ya drinks!" He shouted at them.

The patrons all turned their attentions to their drinks with alacrity and the casual conversation began again. However, it was subdued.

"What's going on Kirkland?" Jim asked him gruffly.

"Well. Charlie's dead," Todd told him bluntly.

"What did you say?"

"I said, Charlie's dead. They found him this morning."

The conversation slowed and they looked again at Jim. They didn't know what to expect but they expected more than this. One of the few people Jim didn't completely despise told him that his nemesis was dead. The feud was over, and he had won. They expected him to dance a hornpipe or jig. Shout with joy or run around like a crazed evangelical. But his face was impassive.

His leg began to tremble, and he shook it once. Jim drained one drink and then the next. He pushed both glasses forward as he stood. Todd walked away pointedly. It was his small way of saying the drinks were free.

"This damn leg has been killing me since the rains, I think I'll go home now."

He said to no one, but at the same time he was addressing the whole bar. All patrons were confused by this behavior, except for Todd Kirkland who knew the circumstances. Which one? He couldn't say and wouldn't be certain. But he could guess.

Jim limped out of the bar to total silence. The old men were stunned by the show of restraint. He whistled once low and slow, and the dog ran after him. They both got into the Patina truck and Jim's leg was trembling. His hand was trembling. He forced his hand and drove home quickly.

When the truck was locked and secure. He and the dog were inside and safe. Jim "boogie" Janson cried. He wept like a child and was angry at that thought and lashed out at the aging house.

He tore photos off the wall and threw tables to the floor. He was angry. Why? He couldn't explain it to himself let alone an outsider. A man who was never soft. Crying. His father would have beaten him. Beat him hard for crying. Maybe that was why he was ashamed. As if his father would rise from the grave after sixty years and beat him now. Beat. He'd won but he felt beat. What's left? What's next? He cried. The last time he cried was in front of his wife as she served him papers. She shamed him and he thought again how his father would have beat him. Maybe should have beat him.

The anger burned the tears away as he ravaged the house. A thousand years prior he could have had a job pillaging. It looked the part as he raged and tore and broke...everything. The dog hid and Jim tore through the house with a vengeance. Whose?

An hour later Jim was sitting on his couch with a cold seven and seven in his slightly trembling hand. The house was broken and torn. The dog looked concerned but still sat close to his friend, on a couch with one cushion. He took a sip of his drink and looked around.

"Alright. I'll admit, that got out of hand."

The dog lifted his head and looked at the old man, as if to say, 'you fucking think?' then lowered his head. Jim slowly shook his head.

"Don't even know where that came from."

The dog cocked his head to the side.

"What the hell do I do now?"

Jim didn't leave the house for the next few weeks except for once to get groceries and once to take the dog to the vet. He missed the funeral. As if he were the type of person to gloat over a grave, he was, but that wasn't the point. Jim just plain didn't see the point of going. Charlie was dead and nothing was gonna change that. Though during the funeral, and without anyone's knowledge but his own, he put his nice suit on and had a 'victory toast'. He called it that, but he knew what it really was.

A lot of people came knocking after Charlie died. Each one offering condolences or congratulations. Sometimes a confused conglomeration of the two. Nobody knew how to act or feel and least of all, Boogie. He obviously turned them all away with the classic, 'fuck off', but they didn't stop. It was starting to get old, older than him and that's a statement.

Two months after Charlie died and Jim was still struggling to find a purpose. He was only mowing his lawn once a week, instead of the customary three to four times a week, depending on the rain. Most days were spent watching tv with the dog.

Getting really into *Wheel...of....*

Ding-Dong.

The doorbell rang. Jim grunted like a rhinoceros getting up off the couch, then cursed like a sailor walking to the door. He was getting ready for his tirade when he opened the door and saw some young punk, he was clearly in his mid-forties. The man was clean shaved and had a healthy smile on his face. His eyes were bright with friendship. What a mistake.

"What the fuck do you want?" Jim asked in Boogie fashion.

The man looked surprised but cleared his throat and carried on.

"Howdy neighbor! I just moved in next door and just wanted to..."

"You a cowboy?"

"Ahem. What, no."

"Oh, right you come up say, fucking *howdy*, to me and now I'm the weird one for asking if you're a cowboy."

"Heh. Yea I guess so," he chuckles nervously.

"You bought Charlie's house?" Jim asked the boy.

"Is Charlie the name of Mr. Stratton? We bought the home from his children."

"Yea his name his was Charlie and he was a stupid fucking prick," the man didn't know what to say so the nervous chuckle continued.

"What's your name?"

"Buddy Lawson and my wife and I just..."

"Your *name* is buddy?"

"Yea and my wife and I..."

"What kind of grown man is named Buddy?"

"Ha-ha...I guess me."

"Can you do me a favor Buddy?"

"Uh, yea, sure."

"Can you go fuck yourself Buddy? I don't talk to children."

SLAM

The door slams heavy and Jim walks away with a smile on his face

The next day Jim woke late per his habit of late but this time he was startled awake by a lawnmower. His first thought was of Charlie and how he would get back at him for waking him up like this. Sugar in the gas-tank maybe or a cart of manure on his front lawn. He was thinking

about his retaliation as he walked to the window and looked down. He saw a young man wearing a shiny shirt pushing a mower haphazardly around Charlie's old yard.

Jim opened the window and yelled down at the man.

"If you want it to not look like shit maybe try going in a straight line!"

The mower stopped and Buddy looks up and smiles.

"Hello, Mr. Janson!"

"What kind of shirt is that? Silk?"

Buddy looks around and then down at his shirt.

"Oh, uh, I think it's polyester."

"Grown men don't wear shiny shirts!"

The window slams with a *thud*.

"Ha! What an idiot. I think I'll go for a drive, you wanna go for a ride boy?"

Four months later Buddy accidentally drove over Jim's flower bed and though he apologized profusely Jim still took it as an act of aggression and declared war. He didn't tell Buddy, but he declared it to himself, and he thought that's all that matters.

That night he snuck over their fence and filled their pool with turtles. The smell the next day in the sun could be smelt for miles. Buddy decided to go old-school, literally, with a juvenile display of penises painted on the sidewalk in front of Jim's house. Jim was mad but he also laughed when no one was looking.

"Think I might pop over to the Buck, come one boy.

The new feud of Buddy and Boogie became the talk of the town. Retaliation, counter-attack, retreat, retaliation, retreat, counter-attack, etc. One day in particular Buddy's wife caught shrapnel fire from the bucket of oatmeal that fell and splattered all over her. Buddy was enfuriated and was borderline ready to come to blows with the old man.

"Listen here you old fuck! Me and you got our own thing going and we'll finish it but you leave my wife out of it!"

"What's the kid gonna do? You gonna hit me? Bah!"

Buddy took aggressive steps forward.

"I just might, at that!'

"You know what?"

"What!"

"I respect that," Jim held his hand out and reluctantly Buddy shook it.

"Yea? Go fuck yourself Jim," Buddy said with a smile.

The term frenemy would apply after that historic moment.

Three years later Jim 'Boogie' Janson died from a heart-attack while trying to push a cart full of manure over to his rival and reluctant friend, Buddy Lawson's house. Buddy saw him and laughed but ran to check on him when he fell. The paramedics pronounced him dead on the scene. Still had a smile on his face.

The kids got the house which they all agreed to promptly sell. They also got whatever was left of the inheritance a sizeable lump but less so divided five ways. They played a video of his last will and testament and in his own words: *"Tell that bitch ex-wife of mine she doesn't get anything. To my ungrateful children, sell the house and split the money and shut the fuck up about it. I want that man-child neighbor of mine to take the dog and the truck. He was mostly a piece of shit, but he wasn't all bad all the time. Take care of both the dog and the truck, I know you will Buddy. To the rest of you, bury me face down so the world can kiss my ass one last time. Ha-ha-ha-ha."*

He continued laughing until the lawyer turned it off, saying, "Alright, that's enough of that."

They held the funeral on a Saturday, 'because fuck em', I want to ruin their weekend' as per Jim's request. Buddy was there, stoic, and struggling to hold back tears. But manly enough not to show it. He knew Jim would have appreciated it. There were many others there that had no problem showing their tears.

Buddy found that surprising until the memorial at the *Salted Buck*, where he heard story after story of how Jim had helped them out at some point or another. The entire town had a similar story. 'Oh, he drove all the way down to Boston just to pick my niece up from Logan, just because my car wouldn't start' or 'He mows all of the widow's homes for free he always said it was just something to do but I think we knew better' everyone had such a story.

Even Buddy had to admit the old man had helped a few times over. Sure, he did it with a smart-ass comment and a few insults sprinkled on top of a healthy pepper of profanity. But he helped without complaint. Well, he always complained he just did it less when someone was in need.

"I guess the old bastard had his own way of helping but it never did stop him from helping did it?" Buddy was talking with Kirkland.

"Molten crust on the outside but a soft gooey center, that's how I'll always remember Boogie," Todd gave a sad smile and slowly bobbed his head as if to agree with himself.

But at the end of the day, Buddy thought, that's exactly how I'll remember him too.

Buddy stood outside of his house with a cup of coffee. The steam blew into the air like an old locomotive on that cold morning. Dammit but he hated to admit that he missed the miserable old bastard. He took a shaky breath of cold morning air and blinked away the tears. The sky was gray and melancholic, not too far from how he felt.

"I can't help but thinking you won this one, you, old fuck," he grimaced and swallowed the lump in his throat with his hot bitter coffee.

The dog whines and he looks down and nods his head.

"Yea boy, I feel the same way," he shakes his head and looks back to the sky.

Buddy was staring at the cold gray sky when he heard a loud truck driving down the road. He squinted in irritation. It's early. Far too early for this shit. The truck rounds a corner and, it's not a truck, just a BMW. The car speeds ahead and a few heartbeats later a U-Haul follows behind. He puts one fist on his hip while the other brings the hot coffee to his lips. He sips and lets the burn fuel his irritation.

The BMW pulls up fast to Boogie's old home and stops with a small squeal. The door opens and expensive leather shoes step out. The man stands and stretches his shoulders underneath a silk shirt? Maybe its polyester? Either way, its shiny and grown men shouldn't wear shiny shirts.

The man's hair is slicked back with far too much gel. He takes off his Italian sunglasses and looks around. He spots Buddy and smiles wide. The man steps forward and onto his lawn. Two steps in Buddy shouts at him,

"Hey, hey! Off the grass, my guy!"

"Oh," the man looks down. "Sorry," he steps back and onto the road again. "I'm your new neighbor, just wanted to say hi,"

"Yea? Do me a favor. Mind your fucking business," Buddy blows on his coffee and walks inside with a small smile on his face. The dog shuffles after him.

About the Author:

Matt White is a novelist who specializes in action, sci-fi, fantasy, adventure, and historical fiction. He is pursuing a BFA in creative writing from Full Sail University. He has his own small online publication called *High Clyde Collaborations* or *HCC*. He enjoys long walks on the beach, spending time with his dogs, drinking pina coladas, and getting caught in the rain.

Website: http://www.hccollab.com

LinkedIn   Profile: https://www.linkedin.com/in/
matt-white-81ba5a233/